W9-BTK-409

Published by Hallmark Gift Books, a division of
Hallmark Cards, Inc., Kansas City, MO 64141

Editor: Chelsea Fogleman
Art Director: Chris Opheim
Designer: Mary Eakin
Production Designer: Bryan Ring

978-1-59530-564-0
SKU: PSB3120

Printed and bound in China
NOV12

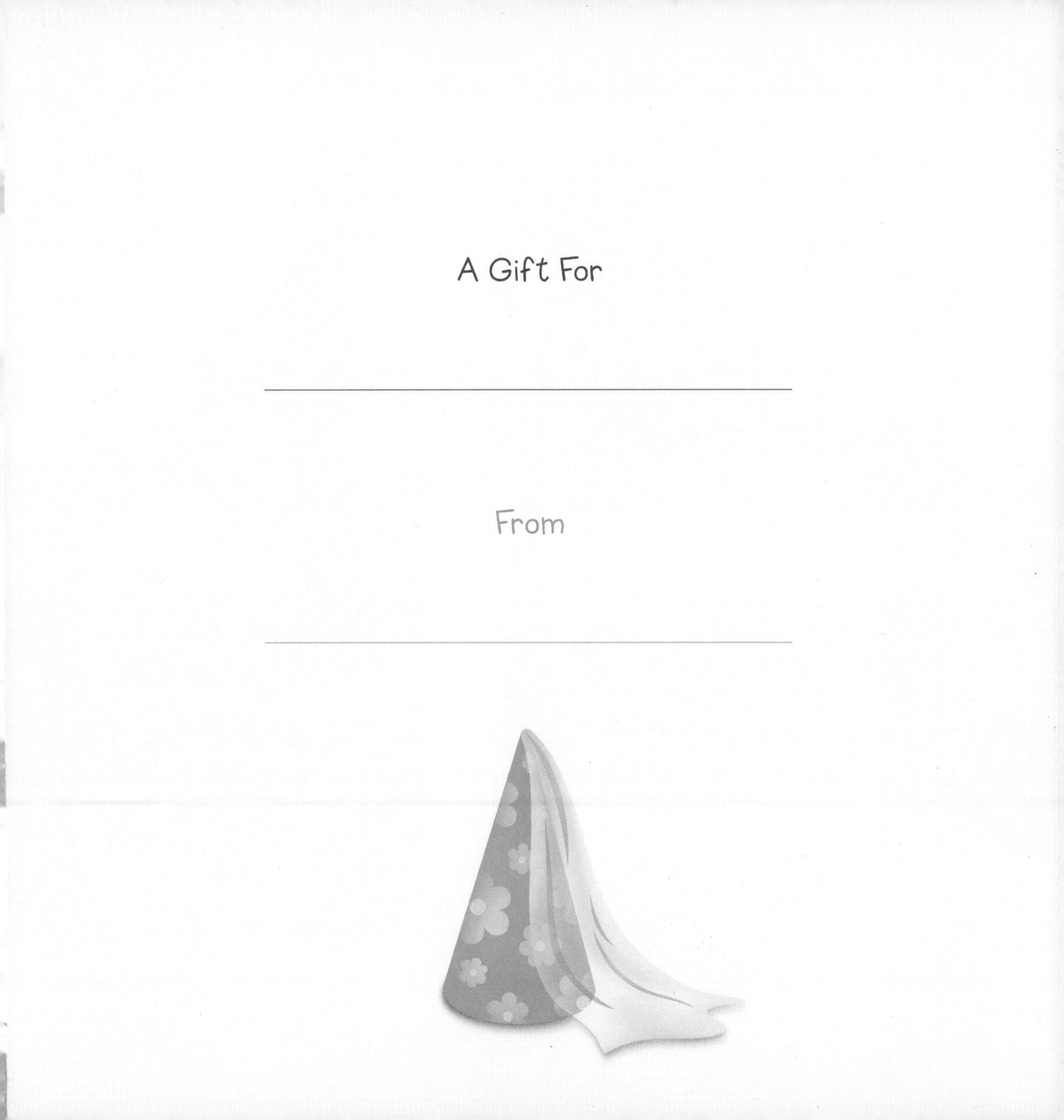
A Gift For
From

How to Use Your Interactive Story Buddy™

1. Activate your Story Buddy by pressing the "On / Off" button on the ear.
2. Read the story aloud in a quiet place. Speak in a clear voice when you see the highlighted phrases.
3. Listen to your Story Buddy respond with several different phrases throughout the book.

Clarity and speed of reading affect the way Posey™ responds. She may not always respond to young children.

Watch for even more Interactive Story Buddy characters. For more information, visit us on the Web at Hallmark.com/StoryBuddy.

Hallmark's **I Reply Technology** brings your Story Buddy™ to life! When you read the key phrases out loud, your Story Buddy™ gives a variety of responses, so each time you read feels as magical as the first.

By Katherine Stano

Illustrated by Maria Sarria

Hallmark

There were all kinds of kittens on Kiki Street. Girly ones. Giggly ones. Goofy ones. Then there was Posey. Posey was a little of everything. She lived in a bright house with a red door. She liked to climb trees, collect postcards, and eat graham crackers with milk. Her favorite day was Saturday. And her favorite class at school was French. She loved to say, "Ooh la la!"

Posey liked lots of stuff, but playing make-believe was the best. Her friends always told her, "Posey, you have a great imagination!"

Posey had fun on her own, but sometimes she liked having a sidekick, too. That was when she'd call in her little brother, Cub, to play along. Cub was good at make-believe, and Posey taught him everything he knew. (She was the big sister, after all.)

It was always exciting to figure out what to play next. Today Posey and Cub ran toward the tree-house castle, shouting, "Let the make-believe begin!"

Posey decided she would play princess. Cub would be castle wizard.

Only, Cub had his own ideas. "I'm an evil troll!" he said.

Posey made a face. She was never a fan of trolls (even the cute ones). "Sorry, Cub. You're a wizard."

But it didn't matter what she said. Cub hobbled around growling like a troll.

"I'm the coolest troll in the land!" Cub sang.

"You're a wizard!" Posey told him.

"Troll."

"WIZARD."

Finally, Cub stomped his foot. "This stinks. If I can't pick what I'm going to be, I don't want to play."

Posey huffed. Oh, what was a girl to do?

So Posey decided to play alone. She practiced her curtsy and waved to her subjects. She even kissed a frog.

But playing by herself was kind of boring. "I know! I'll hang up a welcome banner outside. Maybe someone will pop over for tea. What a marvelous idea."

Posey stood on her toes while the banner flapped in her face. "I can't see anything!" she cried. She wished she had a wizard to help her. (Even a troll might do.) But no such luck!

Then suddenly, a bumblebee buzzed around Posey's head. She was very afraid of bumblebees and leaned against the rail. She couldn't lean much farther, or she would fall. "Oh no!" What was a girl to do?

Suddenly, Cub appeared, waving a lollipop like a magic wand. "Bumblebee, I cast a spell on you!"

He tossed the candy over the rail. The bumblebee flew over the rail, too.

"Cub, you saved the day!" Posey cried. "I have to admit . . . it IS better when you're around. I guess you can be a troll."

Cub shook his head. "Actually, I'm an ogre now."

Posey frowned. Ogres weren't her favorite creatures either. But she was glad to make up with Cub. "All right, Sir Ogre. Come on. Let the make-believe begin."

Just then, there was a loud sound inside the tree house.

"What was that?" Cub gasped.

Posey tiptoed to the doorway. In the corner, she saw a huge shadow.

Cub hid behind his sister. "Ack! A dragon! I can't stand dragon breath!"

Posey kept her cool. "Cub!" she whispered. "Climb on my shoulders!"

Immediately, Cub looked as mighty as a giant. Posey wobbled toward the scary beast. "ROAR!" she shouted.

But the dragon never appeared. Posey was really confused.

Posey and Cub heard a whimper. Then they saw a tiny face peeking up at them.

It was Buttons, Posey's pet mouse. "Oh, Buttons! It's you!" Posey sighed.

Buttons wagged his tail and jumped on Posey. They all toppled to the ground in fits of giggles.

"Hey," said Posey, "Buttons can be a palace pony!" She told Buttons, "I'm the princess, and Cub's an ogre."

Cub chimed in. "Actually, I changed my mind. I'm a troll again. Trolls rule!"

Posey rolled her eyes and put an arm around Cub. Sometimes little brothers kind of ruled, too.

"Okay, evil troll. Let the make-believe begin!"

Did you have fun with Posey™?
We would love to hear from you!

Please send your comments to:

Hallmark Book Feedback

P.O. Box 419034

Mail Drop 215

Kansas City, MO 64141

Or e-mail us at:

booknotes@hallmark.com